P9-DTP-633

Also published by Ruwanga Trading:

The Goodnight Gecko
The Whale Who Wanted to be Small
The Wonderful Journey
A Whale's Tale
The Gift of Aloha
The Shark Who Learned a Lesson
The Brave Little Turtle
Tikki Turtle's Quest
Happy as a Dolphin, *A Child's Celebration of Hawai'i*
How the Geckos Learned to Chirp

First published 1993 by Ruwanga Trading
ISBN 978-0961510275
Printed in China by Everbest Printing Co., Ltd

© 1993 Gill McBarnet

BOOK ENQUIRIES AND ORDERS:
Booklines Hawaii, a division of The Islander Group
269 Pali'i Street
Mililani, Hawaii 96789
Phone: 808-676-0116, ext.206
Fax: 808-676-5156
Toll Free: 1-877-828-4852
Website: www.islandergroup.com

Gecko
Hide and Seek

**written and illustrated by
Gill McBarnet**

On an island,
come and peek. . .
Geckos hide,
and you must seek!

Under a palm tree
near a drum.
Come, oh come. . .
can you find **ONE?**

1

In a field,
    playing peek-a-boo.
Near a pineapple,
    please find **TWO.**

2

High up
  in a mango tree,
Among the leaves
  can you see **THREE?**

3

If you think
  you can find more,
Look in the flowers
  and you'll find **FOUR.**

4

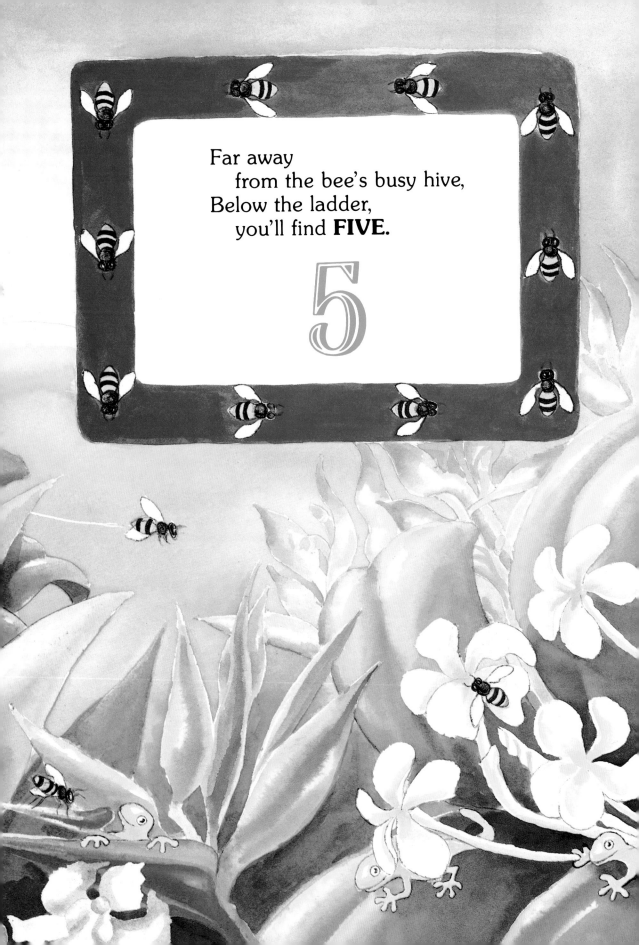

Far away
   from the bee's busy hive,
Below the ladder,
   you'll find **FIVE.**

5

Now find **SIX**,
if you're able.
Look near the chopsticks
on the table.

6

Swimming with tails
going swish, swish, swish. .
Are **SEVEN** small geckos
among the fish.

7

Look nearby
    the brown beach huts.
EIGHT hide near
    the coconuts.

8

Dancing
in a graceful line,
NINE are having
a lovely time!

9

And, what is more,
   that's not all . . .
For **TEN**
   hide near this waterfall.

10

Now that you've found
ONE to **TEN,**
You can add them
up again. . .

1 ONE

2 TWO

3 THREE

4 FOUR

5 FIVE

6 SIX

7 SEVEN

8 EIGHT

9 NINE

10 TEN

Also published by Ruwanga Trading:

The Goodnight Gecko
The Whale Who Wanted to be Small
The Wonderful Journey
A Whale's Tale
The Gift of Aloha
The Shark Who Learned a Lesson
The Brave Little Turtle
Tikki Turtle's Quest
Happy as a Dolphin, *A Child's Celebration of Hawai'i*
How the Geckos Learned to Chirp